P9-BZT-305

Final Sports–Markets
HE TELEGRA
FRIDAY, OCTOBER 30, 1953
PAGES
HOLLYWOOD CALLING
Scouts Scour Country
Benny Go
To Play
Social Notices
Parties
Summon
Goblins
The Halloween witch will have
her broomstick clipped this year—
Search on! Do you fit the Picture?
At The Market Today

North Winds Press
A Division of Scholastic Canada Ltd.

The illustrations for this book were done with coloured pencils and gouache.

Canadian Cataloguing in Publication Data
Muller, Robin
Little wonder

ISBN 0-590-24225-3

I. Title.

PS8576.U55L5 1994 jC813'.54 C93-095603-6
PZ7.M85Li 1994

Text and illustrations copyright © 1994 by Robin Muller.
All rights reserved.
No part of this publication may be reproduced or stored in a retrieval system, or transmitted in any form or by any means, electronic, mechanical, recording, or otherwise, without written permission of the publisher, North Winds Press, a division of Scholastic Canada Ltd., 123 Newkirk Road, Richmond Hill, Ontario, Canada L4C 3G5. In the case of photocopying or other reprographic copying, a licence must be obtained from CANCOPY (Canadian Reprography Collective), 214 King Street West, Suite 312, Toronto, Ontario, M5H 3S6.

6 5 4 3 2 1 Printed in Canada 4 5 6 7 8/9

To Erin and Kael Høecke
and to Sara Porter, the world's only Peruvian Squirrel Hound.

Once, in a big city, there lived an organ grinder named Sylvester and his monkey, Hero. They were partners. Every morning they took their place on a busy street corner. While Sylvester turned the handle of an old-fashioned organ, Hero clowned and did tricks. The crowds cheered Hero's performances and the coins rained down.

At the end of each day, Sylvester and Hero strolled back to their little apartment. "We're like cream cheese on a bagel," Sylvester would say. "All the better for being together!"

LANGLEY

One day, a talent scout saw Hero's performance. "I'll put you in movies, I'll put you on stage, I'll make you a star!" he told the monkey.

Hero somersaulted with excitement.

Sylvester packed Hero's things and said goodbye. "Don't forget to write," he called as the car sped away.

Soon there were pictures of Hero in every magazine and newspaper.

The organ grinder was so proud of his old partner's success that he pinned a big glossy photo of him over the bureau.

Sylvester carried on grinding out the old tunes, but without Hero beside him, no one stopped to toss a coin in his cup.

"If I'm going to earn a living as an organ grinder," Sylvester sighed, "I'd better get another partner."

He went to a pet shop and looked at all the monkeys, but none of them seemed quite right. As he was about to leave, the shop owner stopped him.

"If I can't interest you in a monkey, maybe I can show you something else, something very special." He led the organ grinder to the back of the store.

Palais
PET · SHOP
1962

Trembling inside a cage was a droop-eared, hang-tailed little dog.

"This," said the shop owner, "is a Battersea Boom Beagle, and Battersea Boom Beagles make a sound so unique — why, a forest of songbirds couldn't compete. With a singing dog," he said knowingly, "you'll soon be ankle deep in pennies!"

The little dog looked up at the organ grinder and timidly wagged her tail.

"I'll take her," said Sylvester.

Everyone was astonished to see the organ grinder with a dog instead of a monkey. "She's a Battersea Boom Beagle," Sylvester told the crowd. "And Battersea Boom Beagles make a sound as sweet as a songbird's tweet-tweet. It's lucky for me no one else bought her."

The people were anxious to see the little dog perform. "Does she do tricks?" one asked. "Let's see her clown," another called. "Make her sing,"

they all cried. An old woman held out a penny, but the little dog just cowered behind Sylvester's boot.

"The dog's useless," a voice roared from the crowd. "Little wonder no one wanted it!"

"I wanted her," said Sylvester firmly. "And Little Wonder will be her name. She's a special little dog, just wait and see."

Sylvester showed Little Wonder all of Hero's tricks. He scampered, bounced and stood on his head. He somersaulted, walked on his hands and rolled his eyes. He even twirled a coin on the end of his nose, but the little dog just sat and stared.

"Won't you even sing?" pleaded Sylvester. "That's what Battersea Boom Beagles *do*." He demonstrated by wailing to the music of the organ, but Little Wonder didn't make a sound.

"I'm going to prove that you *are* a little wonder," said Sylvester, "even if I have to change the act!" The organ grinder tried new songs and new costumes — he even tried changing places with the little dog. Nothing worked.

HERE
HERO
YING

Together they earned barely enough to pay the rent, and many nights they went hungry. On those nights Sylvester would look longingly at the picture of Hero and sigh.

Soon Sylvester became ill. He shivered and coughed and was too weak to get out of bed.

The neighbours grew concerned. "He needs some chicken soup," said one. "He needs a mustard plaster," said another. "He needs a doctor," said a third. So they called a doctor, who called an ambulance, which took Sylvester to the hospital. They were so busy that they forgot all about Little Wonder.

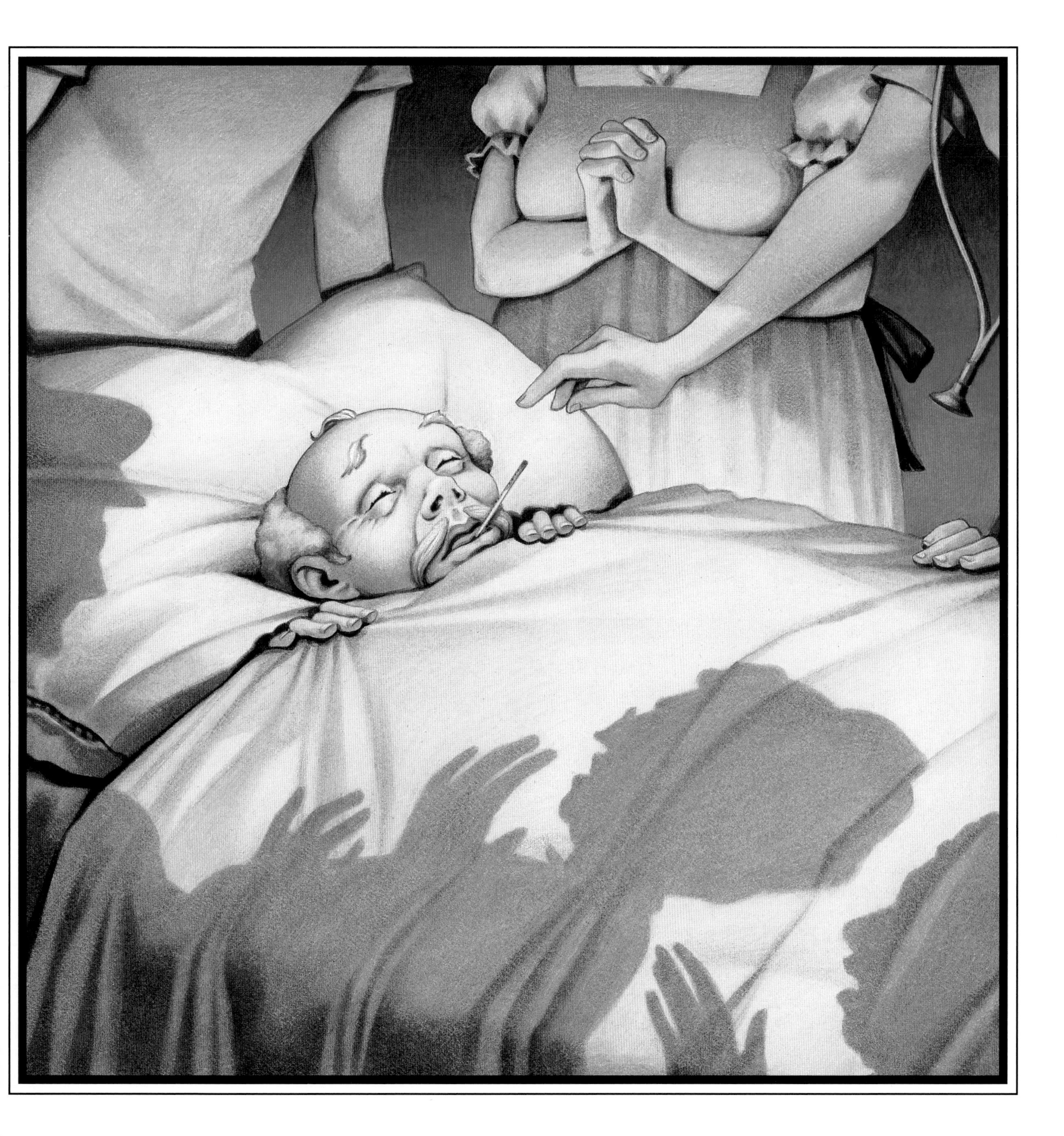

When everyone had left, Little Wonder peeked out from under a chair. She sniffed around, but Sylvester was gone. Little Wonder missed the organ grinder. She missed the way he would twirl, bounce and stand on his head. She missed the way he would walk on his hands, somersault and roll his eyes. She missed the way he would wail loudly at the sound of the organ. But most of all, she missed curling up on Sylvester's lap in the evening. She loved Sylvester and wondered when he would return home.

Little Wonder stared at the door and listened. The rain fell. Cars and trucks rumbled by. An alley cat screeched in the darkness.

All night Little Wonder waited.

HERO

In the morning, the rain stopped and the sun came out. Milk trucks passed, bottles clinking. Children laughed. The day grew warm. And Little Wonder waited.

Horns honked. Mothers called their children for dinner. An ice cream vendor rang his bell. And Little Wonder waited.

Evening came. Men stood on the corner and talked. Radios blared. Parents sang their children to sleep. And still Little Wonder waited.

Soon it was dark and everything grew still. Little Wonder sat, motionless, waiting by the door. Suddenly something jiggled in the lock. The knob turned and the door swung open. Sylvester had come home!

Overjoyed, Little Wonder was about to run to the figure in the doorway, but something stopped her. It *wasn't* the organ grinder.

The little dog shrank back into the shadows as a burglar stepped into the room.

The man yanked open cupboards, overturned the bed and emptied the drawers. He took everything, even Sylvester's organ. The burglar was about to leave when something caught his eye. Little Wonder watched as the man snatched the photo of Hero from the wall and stuffed it into his sack.

Little Wonder knew she had to stop the intruder. But what could she do against such a big man? Little Wonder thought of Sylvester and she mustered all her courage.

As the burglar turned to leave, Little Wonder bounded into the light, prancing wildly at the man's feet. The burglar was so startled that he lost his balance, coming down with a crash. Little Wonder didn't waste a moment. She twirled, bounced and stood on her head. Then she walked on her front paws, somersaulted and rolled her eyes.

The man roared with anger. "Beat it, you screwy mutt!" he yelled, and kicked Little Wonder into a corner.

Clutching the sack, the burglar stumbled to the door. There was only one thing left to do. Opening her mouth, Little Wonder let out a sound. The sound was not like a songbird's sweet tweet. It was not like the sound that Sylvester made when singing. It was a sound that began deep and rumbling and came out full, round and booming, the kind of sound Battersea Boom Beagles are famous for.

The blast shook the building. Windows rattled, pictures fell and sleepers were thrown from their beds. "It's an earthquake, it's a volcano!" they yelled. "Call the police! Call the fire department! Call my mother!" They called all three.

Soon the street was filled with police cars and fire trucks. When the rescuers searched the building they found Little Wonder sitting on the stunned burglar, the contents of his sack scattered on the floor beside them.

As the man was led away by the police, he shouted out, "That dog's a siren, a horn and a blasted burglar alarm rolled into one! It oughta be locked up!"

Little Wonder was the talk of the town. The newspaper printed a picture of her cradled in Sylvester's arms. The headline read "Booming Beagle Bags Burglar."

"I always knew you had it in you!" chuckled Sylvester. "From now on we're going to be like chicken soup with rice. Together forever." Little Wonder wagged her tail.

When Sylvester came home he gave up being an organ grinder. Instead, he and Little Wonder made their fortune selling toy Battersea Boom Beagles that twirled, bounced, rolled their eyes — and when they opened their mouths, made a sound so loud it blew your hat off.

54 PAGES
High 60
Details Page Two
WARMING UP
THURSDAY, MAY 6, 1954
BOOMING BEAGLE
BAGS BURGLAR
MOVIESTAR MONKEY
NABBED IN
BANANA BAR BRAWL
A HAPPY REUNION
Teachers Welcomed
Telegraph Fashion Reporter
by His Honor the Lieutenant
latter in black, with